GH STBUSTERS

Adapted by John Sazaklis · Illustrated by Alan Batson

Based on the Screenplay Written by Dan Aykroyd and Harold Ramis
Directed by Ivan Reitman

A GOLDEN BOOK · NEW YORK

Ghostbusters TM & © 2016 Columbia Pictures Industries, Inc. All Rights Reserved. Published in the United States
by Golden Books, an imprint of Random House Children's Books, a division of Penguin Random House LLC,
1745 Broadway, New York, NY 10019, and in Canada by Penguin Random House Canada Limited, Toronto.
Golden Books, A Golden Book, A Little Golden Book, the G colophon, and the distinctive gold spine
are registered trademarks of Penguin Random House LLC.
randomhousekids.com
Educators and librarians, for a variety of teaching tools, visit us at RHTeachersLibrarians.com
ISBN 978-1-5247-1489-5 (trade) — ISBN 978-1-5247-1490-1 (ebook)
Printed in the United States of America
10 9 8 7 6 5 4 3 2

When there's something strange haunting you, like ghosts and spooks and specters, and things that go bump in the night . . . **"Who you gonna call?"**

THE GHOSTBUSTERS!

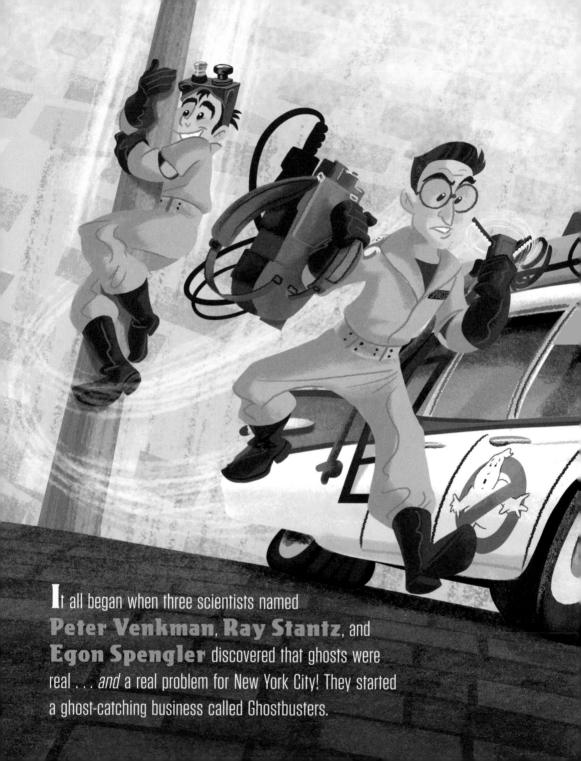

It all began when three scientists named
Peter Venkman, **Ray Stantz**, and
Egon Spengler discovered that ghosts were
real . . . *and* a real problem for New York City! They started
a ghost-catching business called Ghostbusters.

When the alarm rings, they grab their proton packs and ghost traps. Then they race to the scene of the disturbance in their souped-up ghostbusting-mobile, **Ecto-1**.

The Ghostbusters realized that things were getting a little weird when they answered a call at a fancy uptown hotel. Ray spotted something he'd never seen before—a hungry green ghost named **SLIMER**.

Ray chased Slimer right into Peter—

Using his **PKE** (psychokinetic energy) meter, Egon tracked Slimer to the hotel's ballroom. Egon warned the Ghostbusters not to cross their proton packs' streams. "It would be bad," he explained.

This ghost is toast!

The Ghostbusters quickly snared Slimer in a tangle of proton beams and sucked him into one of their traps!

Soon more and more ghosts appeared, scaring up trouble all over town.

Peter, Ray, and Egon needed help, so they hired a man named **Winston Zeddemore**. Winston chased ghosts across the city as a Ghostbuster!

But where were all the ghosts coming from . . . ?

The answer to that question could be found uptown. A supernatural cloud above a high-rise apartment building was drawing in ghosts from another dimension!

One day, a young musician named **Dana Barrett** was resting in her apartment. Suddenly, her favorite chair came to life and tried to grab her!

And Dana's neighbor, accountant **Louis Tully**, almost became the chew toy of a snarling **Terror Dog**!

Something very strange was happening!

The Ghostbusters rushed to the rescue! At the top of the building, they found Dana and Louis—and a powerful being named **Gozer**!

"Whatever it is, it will have to get past us!" Peter declared.

Suddenly, Gozer transformed Dana and Louis into two growling Terror Dogs with glowing red eyes! Then the villain exclaimed,

"Choose the form of the Destructor!"

The Ghostbusters fired proton beams at Gozer, but it vanished into thin air. Suddenly, a spooky voice boomed, **"The choice is made!"**

"Whoa!" Peter shouted, looking at his teammates. "Did you choose anything?"

"I . . . I just couldn't help it," Ray stammered.

LOOK!

Ray hadn't meant to, but he had thought of it. Now the Destructor
had taken the form of a marshmallow man hundreds of feet tall!
"There's something you don't see every day," Peter joked as the giant
marched toward them.

The Stay Puft Marshmallow Man climbed the building, reaching out with his delicious puffy hand to grab the Ghostbusters!

Egon came up with a radical idea: "We'll cross the streams."
The Ghostbusters combined the streams from their proton packs into
one massive blast . . . and aimed it right into the portal Gozer had opened.

Heat from the explosion roasted the Stay Puft Marshmallow Man. Everything was covered in fluffy white goo. But it had worked—
the portal was closed.

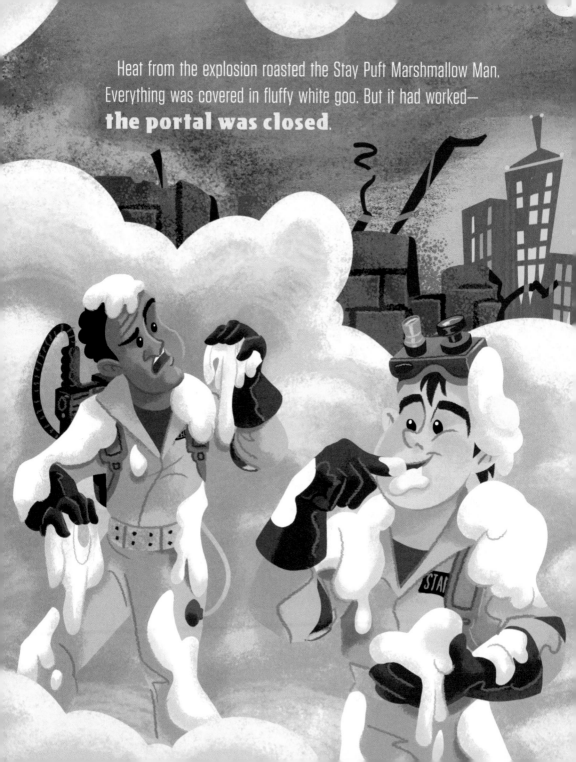

Dana and Louis returned to normal, and the city was saved!

The heroes were greeted by thousands of cheering fans.

"I love this town!" Winston said.

Now the city knew exactly who to call—

THE GHOSTBUSTERS!